BATMAN ™
IS LOYAL

written by
CHRISTOPHER HARBO

illustrated by
GREGG SCHIGIEL

BATMAN created by
Bob Kane with
Bill Finger

PICTURE WINDOW BOOKS
a capstone imprint

Batman is loyal. He supports his friends and protects his city. The people of Gotham City can trust him to help them.

When Gotham City is under attack,
Batman rises to defend it.

The Dark Knight is loyal because he always keeps his city safe.

When Batman makes a promise, he always follows through.

Batman is loyal because he keeps his word.

When criminals cause chaos, the Caped Crusader leaps into battle.

Batman is loyal because he doesn't let fear get in his way.

When Robin trains, Batman serves as his coach.

The Caped Crusader is loyal because he believes in his friends.

When the Justice League calls, Batman joins its mission.

Batman is loyal because he always supports his team.

When Ace the Bat-Hound needs his daily exercise, Batman takes him for a run.

The Dark Knight is loyal because he follows through with his responsibilities.

When Batgirl asks for backup,
Batman stands watch.

Batman is loyal because he does
what he's asked.

When the Caped Crusader takes on trouble, he battles to the very end.

Batman is loyal because he finishes what he starts.

Whenever Batman swoops in, villains run for cover.

For they know, above all, Batman is
loyal to justice!

BATMAN SAYS...

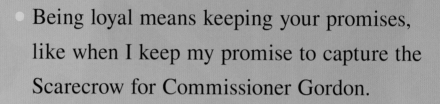

- Being loyal means defending your community and country, like when I protect Gotham City from the Penguin's attack.

- Being loyal means keeping your promises, like when I keep my promise to capture the Scarecrow for Commissioner Gordon.

- Being loyal means believing in your friends, like when I coach Robin to become a better crime-fighter.

- Being loyal means always supporting your team, like when I help the Justice League defeat the Injustice Gang.

- Being loyal means being the very best you that you can be!

GLOSSARY

chaos (KAY-oss)—total confusion

defend (di-FEND)—to try to keep someone or something from being changed or harmed

exercise (EK-suhr-syz)—a physical activity done in order to stay healthy and fit

justice (JUHSS–tiss)—the system of laws in a country

mission (MISH-uhn)—a planned job or task

promise (PROM-iss)—your word that you will do something

protect (pruh-TEKT)—to keep safe

support (suh-PORT)—to help and encourage someone

trust (TRUHST)—to believe someone is honest and reliable

READ MORE

Harbo, Christopher. *Batman Is Trustworthy*. DC Super Heroes Character Education. North Mankato, Minn.: Capstone Press, 2018.

Nelson, Robin. *Am I a Good Friend?: A Book About Trustworthiness*. Show Your Character. Minneapolis: Lerner Publications Company, 2014.

Pettiford, Rebecca. *Being Honest*. Building Character. Minneapolis: Jump Inc., 2018.

INTERNET SITES

FactHound offers a safe, fun way to find Internet sites related to this book. All of the sites on FactHound have been researched by our staff.

Here's all you do:

Visit *www.facthound.com*

Type in this code: 9781515840190

DC Super Heroes Character Education
is published by Picture Window Books
A Capstone Imprint
1710 Roe Crest Drive
North Mankato, Minnesota 56003
www.mycapstone.com

STAR41226

Editor: Julie Gassman
Designer: Charmaine Whitman
Art Director: Hilary Wacholz
Colorist: Rex Lokus

Cataloging-in-Publication Data is available
on the Library of Congress website.

ISBN: 978-1-5158-4019-0 (library binding)
ISBN: 978-1-5158-4284-2 (paperback)
ISBN: 978-1-5158-4023-7 (eBook PDF)

Printed and bound in India.
002620